C ss

leapfrog

Rhyme
Time

Giraffe's
Good Game

First published in 2008 by
Franklin Watts
338 Euston Road
London
NW1 3BH

Franklin Watts Australia
Level 17/207 Kent Street
Sydney
NSW 2000

A CIP catalogue record for this book is available
from the British Library.

ISBN 978 0 7496 7944 6 (hbk)
ISBN 978 0 7496 7956 9 (pbk)

Series Editor: Jackie Hamley
Series Advisor: Dr Barrie Wade
Series Designer: Peter Scoulding

Printed in China

Franklin Watts is a division of
Hachette Children's Books,
an Hachette Livre UK company.

Giraffe's Good Game

by Margaret Nash

Illustrated by Bruno Robert

FRANKLIN WATTS
LONDON•SYDNEY

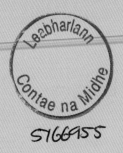

Giraffe was fed up.

His legs were too long.

He thought he was clumsy
and did everything wrong.

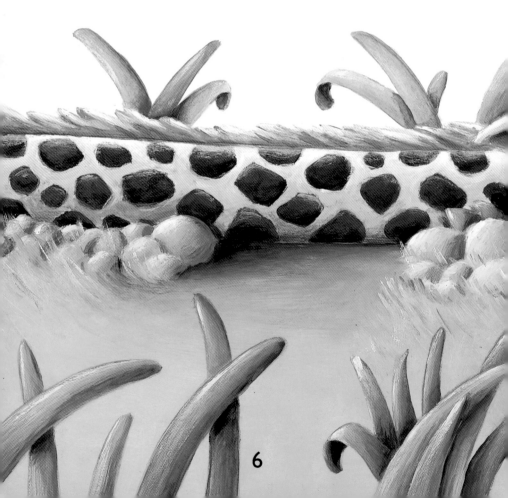

The others had fun
playing games every day.

But when Giraffe joined in, he got in the way.

"Why don't you try this?"
his friend Monkey said,

as he rolled over and
stood on his head.

Giraffe did his best,
but he got in a muddle.

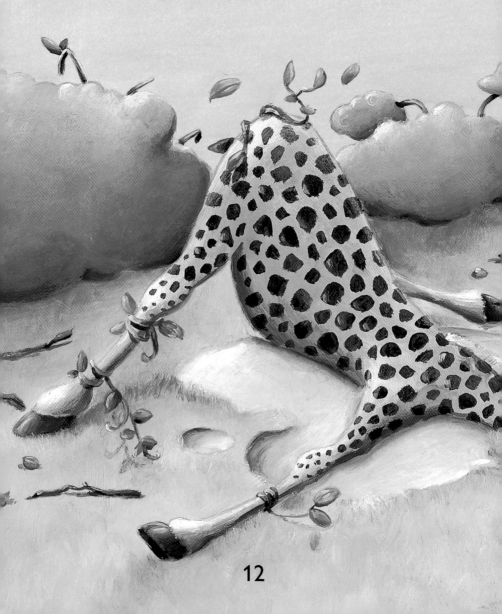

His legs tangled up
and he fell in a puddle.

They tried

Hide and Seek ...

15

... but that was no good.

He got found too quickly
wherever he stood!

They played
Hunt the Pebble ...

... but Giraffe was too tall.
His head was too high up
to see things so small.

21

"Let's climb trees!"
the babies all cried.
They loved to climb up,
and look down from the sky.

And only Giraffe
was able to see
that the babies climbed
too high up in the tree.

The scared babies cried,
"Help! We're stuck
up here!"

Then clever Giraffe
had a brilliant idea.

"Slide down my long neck!"
Giraffe quickly said.
The babies jumped down,
one by one, on his head.

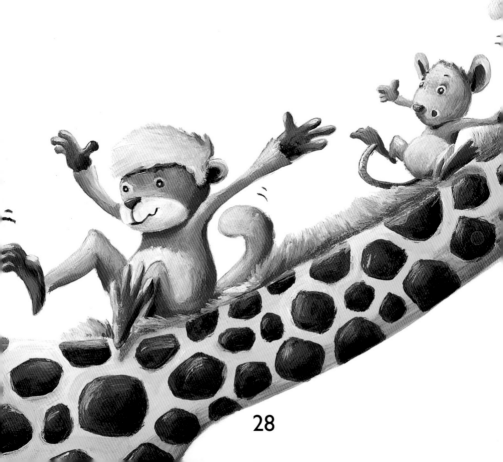

"Whee!" said the babies.
"This is good fun!"
And that's how Giraffe's
Good Game was begun!

Leapfrog Rhyme Time has been specially designed to fit the requirements of the Literacy Framework. It offers real books for beginner readers by top authors and illustrators. There are 27 Leapfrog Rhyme Time stories to choose from: